The Exiles

D1362766

The Exiles

The Exiles

IAIN CRICHTON SMITH

Poetry Book Society

Acknowledgements are due to: the *Stornoway Gazette*: *PN Review*:
the *Listener*: the *Scotsman*: *New Poetry* edited by Douglas Dunn:
the BBC: *Stand*: *Encounter*: *The Times Literary Supplement*:
Lines Review: *Equivalences*.

First published in 1984 by

Carcanet Press Ltd
210 Corn Exchange Buildings
Manchester M4 3BQ

Raven Arts Press
31 North Frederick St
Dublin 1

British Library Cataloguing in Publication Data
Smith, Iain Crichton
The Exiles.
I. Title
821'.914   PR6005.R58

ISBN 0-85635-495-3 (Carcanet)
ISBN 0-906897-73-4 (Raven Arts)

*The publisher acknowledges the financial assistance of
the Arts Council of Great Britain*

Printed in England by SRP Ltd., Exeter

CONTENTS

THE EXILES

RETURNING EXILE

You who come home do not tell me
anything about yourself, where you have come from,
why your coat is wet, why there is grass in your hair.

The sheep huddle on the hills as always,
there's a yellow light as if cast by helmets,
the fences made of wire are strung by the wind.

Do not tell me where you have come from, beloved stranger.
It is enough that there is light still in your eyes,
that the dog rising on his pillar of black knows you.

THERE IS NO SORROW

There is no sorrow worse than this sorrow
the dumb grief of the exile
among villages that have strange names
among the new rocks.
The shadows are not his home's shadows
nor the tales his tales
and even the sky is not the same
nor the stars at night.

Sometimes he sees his home in the stars
the light from its window
his village trembling and vibrating
and the old white faces
mumbling at the fire.

But the strange names stand up against him
and the dryness of the earth
and the cold barks of dogs
and his sails are folded in this harbour
which is not his.

Poor lost exile
For you there is nothing but endurance
till one miraculous day
you will wake up in the morning
and put on your foreign clothes
and know that they are at last yours.

NEXT TIME

Listen, when you come home
to see your wife again
where the tapestry stands unfinished
across the green brine,
sit among the stones
and consider how it was
in the old days
before you became a king
and walked hunchbacked
with decisions on your shoulders.

Sit among the rocks
hearing the sound of the sea
eternally unchanging
and watch the butter-cups
so luminously pale.

The cries of the dead
haunt the gaunt headland
and the shields clash
in that astonishing blue.

Simply enter the boat
and leave the island
for there is no return,
boy, forerunner of kings.

Next time, do this,
salt bronzed veteran
let the tapestry be unfinished
as truthful fiction is.

RETURNING EXILE

Home he came after Canada
Where for many years he drank
his failure into the ground.
Westward lay Lewis. He never wrote.
The snow needs a gay pen.
However at the age of fifty-five
he put on his hat, his painted tie,
and packed his trunk, being just alive.
Quietly he sailed over waters
through which he saw his home all green
and salmon leaping between deer's horns.
Arrived home he attended church,
the watch-chain snaking his waistcoat.
No one was as black or stiff as he.
He cast his bottles into outer darkness
where someone gnashed his teeth
each evening by the quay
watching the great ship sail out
with the girls laughing
the crew in white
and the bar mazy with mirrors.
Some called her SS. Remorse,
others the bad ship Envy.

THE EXILES

(translated from the author's own Gaelic)

The many ships that left our country
with white wings for Canada.
They are like handkerchiefs in our memories
and the brine like tears
and in their masts sailors singing
like birds on branches.
That sea of May running in such blue,
a moon at night, a sun at daytime,
and the moon like a yellow fruit,
like a plate on a wall
to which they raise their hands
like a silver magnet
with piercing rays
streaming into the heart.

WHEN MY POETRY MAKING HAS FAILED

When my poetry making has failed
I sit in the middle of autumn like a black clock
uselessly ticking.
I try to sing
inside my glazed armour,
a tortoise on fire.
But nothing saves me except for the water that runs
harmlessly and without herald
from some place that I have been and cannot remember
where the words stand around like rocks.

ALWAYS

Always in the same way the poets die
when the girls on horses irretrievably
cross the horizons that are slowly closed,

when the ravens no longer dip their pens in ink
and the winds bring no treasures from the west
in stubbly autumn, of sharp absences:

when cafés that in corners once were lit
round pale-faced waitresses tenderly subside
to pavements crowded with bowler hats and furs;

and the manuscripts of spring are whirled away
from cloaks of the sad monks and thinner nuns
when prayers are points of meagre icicles,

and the late evening skies are lost sails
beyond all feeling's mercy, beyond lights
trembling and yellow of the unmown wake.

IN THE SPRING

In the spring, air returns to us,
wide, with a sense of windows,

and our ruinous virtues sparkle once more
like old cans in a ditch.

On such a day Hector set out
in leaf upon leaf of blue

in the spring that surged windily over Troy,
its banks with their whipped green swords,

before the fire sizzled, and the bones were given to the dogs,
and the sea pink reddened the shore.

SPEECH FOR A WOMAN

One night
I saw my children
climbing the stairs in the frost

which had carved an unintelligible language
on the single window.

'Where have you been?' I asked
for they were whistling
and talking about the magic games they had played
in green ferocious shirts.

'Everywhere,' they said.
'Especially where the blue sky blackens
under the weight of the seas:
and particularly in a desert from which we saw
a woman in a brown shawl waving.
Ships we took, trains we took, and the green buses
that flowed across a country under siege
where the same women with their empty mouths
spoke of eternal famine.'

The whistling faded.
I opened their room.
It was tidier than I had ever seen it.

The sweaty socks were not to be seen
nor the embroidered jerseys,
nor the records with the satanic drums
nor the pictures.

It was a ruined shrine that I was looking at.
Slowly the clock began to tick

And it flowed through my whole body
which was a dress of sand
emptying like an hourglass as I gazed.

YOUTH

When the wind blows the curtains wide, do you not
 remember
the green trams on their wires and yourself young
singing on a street that no one now can find.

It is as if the book opens, showing the parts you have played
in a theatre more precious to you than the Globe
with its ghostly flag flying in an Elizabethan wind.

WHEN THEY REACHED THE NEW LAND

When they reached the new land they rebuilt the old one,
they called the new mountains by old names,

they carved a Presbyterian church on the hill.
Nevertheless there was a sort of slantness,

a curious odd feeling in the twilight
that the mountain had shifted, had cast off its name

and even the Christ in the window seemed different
as if he had survived deserts and was not

a shepherd whom they imagined with his sheep
and his long staff high on the rainy hills.

It was much later before they made it all fit
and by then it was a new land.

They could have changed the names of the mountains
and could have walked in the familiar streets

built by their own strivings. It was then
that their old land was swallowed by the new;

and Christ a haunter of their own deserts,
the birds the colourful haunters of their own

trees and gardens. And they were at peace
among their settled, naturalised names.

EARLY AUSTRALIAN

If the cards should turn out right, let your butler
follow you with his tray, letters from home,
and bend his back among the foreign names.
Otherwise let all things be unpronounceable.
Sink into the gibberish and make no sense,
outcast of lawns, inhabitant of eerie heaven.

AUSTRALIA

1

In Australia the trees are deathly white,
the kangaroos are leaping halfway to heaven
but land at last easily on the earth.
Sometimes I hear graves singing
their Gaelic songs to the dingos
which scrabble furiously at the clay.
Then tenderly in white they come towards me,
drifting in white, the far exiles
buried in the heart of brown deserts.
It is a strange language they speak
not Australian not Gaelic
while the green eyes stalk them
under a moon the same as ours
but different, different.

2

Naturally there are photographs of Ned Kelly
in his iron mask in his iron armour.
His iron body hung stiffly in the wind
which blew past the ravens.
In that dry land his armour will not rust
and the hot sun flashes from it
as if it were a mirror, creator of fresh stars.
However dingos leap at it they will not chew him
for he is a story, a poem,
a tale that is heard on the wind.

3

No, you will not return from Australia
However you may wish to do so.
For you have surrendered to its legend,
to its music being continually reborn,

to the eerie whine of its deserts.
Somehow or another it entered your soul
and however much you remember Scotland,
its graves sanctified by God,
its historical darknesses,
you will not return from it.
Its dust is in your nostrils,
its tenderness has no justice,
its millions of stars are the thoughts
of unbridled horsemen.
With blue eyes you will stare
blinded into its blueness
and when you remember your rivers,
the graveyards the mountains,
it is Australia that stands up in front of you,
your question, your love.

4

All day the kookaburra is laughing
from the phantoms of trees,
from the satire of nature.
It is not tragedy nor comedy,
it is the echo of beasts,
the bitter chorus of thorns,
and flowers that have names
that aren't easily remembered.
The kookaburra laughs from the trees,
from the branches of ghosts,
but the sky remains blue
and the eyes glow green in the night.

THE MAN WITHOUT A NAME

He exists somewhere, perhaps in America,
this man who was once a beast.

The postman does not bring his name
or his address
or the mint scent of Prussia.

He bolts his door at night, speaks little,
lest his accent betray him,
lest suddenly he wear the grey
uniform of ash.

What a life, what a sorrow,
what a grief,
in this naive land
where Nixon cried and laughed easily,
'Love me, love my dog.'

How understand them,
their cleanliness,
their tanned long-legged girls,
bred on Coca Cola,
springing from cafés.

Evil is an ancient mould
that grows from weariness.
Only Poe knew of it
in this new country,

where conversation passes you like water
and the fountains are playing
in squares which you visit each day
to sit on a bench.

Nameless abhorred wanderer!
The Wandering Jew!
What pathos there is in autumn,
what turbulence in spring,
the furnace of summer.

Someday someone will accost you
and call you by your new name
which you've stamped on your passport.
'Hey, Ted,' he'll say,
'Didn't I know you in Europe
forty years ago?'

And something will stand at attention
before the furnace.
'Herr,' you will say, might say,
'I surrender.
I want like those others to get
my own name back.'

'I am tired of the trains that pass
each day with their freight
carriage after carriage racing
towards the factories.
Take the gold from my teeth
the watch from my wrist
the medal from my shirt
take the stiffness out of my back
and the ring
from my German hand,
take the children from my wallet
for I want my name to burn
in this American air.'

PRINCE CHARLES

To the Highlands he came, boyishly running.
There was clear water there, greenery without form,
a waste of stones, nature's academy.

And so adventurously he rode and fought.
This was a fresh land to put his stamp on.
This was in the end his hoped-for home.

He marched and marched and then turned back and marched.
The dizzying snow blossomed against his face.
He was the ghost so powder-white and dumb.

He turned away, his horse obscured by snow,
his torn shirt a sail, the sun so warm
and still adventurous on his secret boat.

But he fattened steadily far from that gaunt waste.
To love a home is not to find it true.
He drank and drank in that intriguing blue

of Italy, the rich luxurious land.
Thin sheep cropped the rocks, the tinkling streams
flowed to the sea, the port, the bitter wine.

NO RETURN

No, really you can't go back to
that island any more. The people
are growing more and more unlike you
and the fairy stories
have gone down to the grave in peace.

The wells are dry now and the long grasses
parched by their mouths, and the horned cows
have gone away to another country
where someone else's imagination
is fed daily on milk.

There were, you remember, sunsets
against which the black crows were seen
and a moonlight of astonishing beauty
calmed at midnight by waters
which you're not able to hear.

The old story-telling people
have gone home to their last houses
under the acres of a lost music.
These have all been sold now
to suave strangers with soft voices.

It is a great pity that your cottage
preserved in January by clear ice
and in June surrounded by daisies
has been sold to the same strangers
and the bent witches evicted.

If you were to return now the roofs
would appear lower, the walls would have no echoes,
the wavelike motion would be lost,

the attics where you read all day
would be crammed with antiques.

No, you cannot return to an island
expecting that the dances will be unchanged,
that the currency won't have altered,
that the mountains blue in the evening
will always remain so.

You can't dip your mouth in the pure spring
ever again or ever again be haunted
by the 'eternal sound of the ocean'.
Even the boats which you once rowed
have set off elsewhere.

The witches wizards harlequins jesters
have packed up their furniture and guitars.
The witches have gone home on their broomsticks
and the conjurors with their small horses
and tiny carts have departed

leaving the island bare, bleak and windy,
itself alone in its barren corner
composed of real rocks and real flowers
indifferent to the rumours and the stories
stony, persistent.

THE NEW HOUSES

Across the road they are building new flats,
the men in red helmets and red oilskins.
I'm eighty-seven years old. It's a fresh morning
in my adopted country of Canada.
The radio is burbling all day long.
Soon I'll be buried here far from home.
Yesterday on the road I saw two snails,
one green, one black, the green one ate the other.
And I've seen a green snake at the door.
In this garden my wife planted a rose
which I water, daily, with green snaky hosepipe.
Two years she's dead and heaven is possible.
I believe in God and in his foreign mansions.
Sometimes I dream of Lewis in the night,
of the sails that slanted towards Canada
of the wild geese I shot above the marshes
where now are houses, near the big Pacific,
on the sands of which fat men are practising baseball.
I shall be buried here, that's for sure.
It's nice to hear the sound of the hammers
and to see the men in their red helmets
as if not one but many suns are rising
over this land, my own, yet somehow different.

HOME

Home from Zimbabwe you look tired and ill
after your half-hour walk to help your heart
in Helensburgh not seen for thirty years.
The promenade, the sea, the changing cafés,
when you and your wife met when she was a girl,
and you a lieutenant in the last World War,
before you entered specious history
and lived in a spacious garden for a while
among the blacks with their first bicycles.
The lights are blue and strange in this late chill
after the weather of Rhodesia,
after the yachts that glittered in this bay,
the tangly seaweed and the morning haze.
'Where will you go?' I ask. You wearily say,
'A possible place would be America.
My wife says Britain's much too cold for her.'
To become at sixty a late wanderer!
So much has happened. Puzzled, you fall quiet,
and all I hear's the foghorn from the sea
and your slight lame breathing in the living room

READING SHAKESPEARE

On a dark day in winter I read Shakespeare.
The birds set off to branches of the south.
I tremble in the branches of the mind.

Summer is finished. Shakespeare always remains,
tree on tree for ever fragrant, young,
leaves that never fall out of the leaves.

Forest of Arden, you are my best south,
the lightning wit in this locality,
the cloudless sky, the rainbow tunics there,

and thunder too. We have the best of it,
so many weathers, changeable, intense.
Farewell to the long-necked geese that cross the sea.

SPEECH FOR PROSPERO

When I left that island I thought I was dead. Nothing
stirred in me. Miranda in jeans
and totally innocent was standing by a sail
and all the others happily recovered talking
in suits made of brine. But to return to
the gossip, the poisonous ring, was not easy,
and many times I nearly tried to turn back
feeling in my bones the desolate hum of the headland,
my creation of rivers and mist.
Still we went on. The corruption had put on flesh,
the young were hopeful again, all was forgiven.
Nevertheless the waiters were scraping and bowing,
the rumours beginning, the crowns of pure crystal were
      sparkling,
the telephones were ringing with messages from the grave
and the thin phosphorescent boys glowing with ambition
in corners of velvet and death.
Still I went on. The ship left its wake behind it,
shining and fading, cord of a new birth,
and over by the rail Miranda gazed at her prince
yearning for love.
Goodbye, island, never again shall I see you,
you are part of my past. Though I may dream of you often
I know there's a future we all must learn to accept,
music working itself out in the absurd halls and the mirrors,
posturings of men like birds, Art in a torrent of plates,
the sound of the North Wind, distant yet close,
as stairs ascend from the sea.

'YOU'LL TAKE A BATH'

'And now you'll take a bath,' she'd always say,
just when I was leaving, to keep me back.
At the second turning of the stony stair
the graffiti were black letters in a book
misspelt and menacing. As I drove away
she'd wave from the window. How could I always bear
to be her knight abandoning her to her tower
each second Sunday, a ghost that was locked fast
in a Council scheme, where radios played all day
unknown raw music, and young couples brought
friends home to midnight parties, and each flower
in the grudging garden died in trampled clay.

Standing by her headstone in the mild
city of bell-less doors, I feel the sweat
stink my fresh shirt out, as each gravelly path
becomes a road, long lost, in a bad bet.
Once more I see the dirty sleepy child.
'The water's hot enough. You'll have a bath.'

And almost I am clean but for that door
so blank and strong, imprinted with her name
as that far other in the scheme was once,
and 'scheme' becomes a mockery, and a shame,
in this neat place, where each vase has its flower,
and the arching willow its maternal stance.

CINDERELLA

Always in rough cloth she scrubs the floor.
She dreams to be as elegant as her sisters
who sit in state, dream of yet higher things.

The floor's the mirror where they see their dreams.
If they could see it in its nakedness
the soul might rid them of such lavishness.

There's danger in the coach and in the shoe
as much as in the sisters' relishings.
Fantasy's the food that the soul dreads

preferring simple stool and simple tale,
as anchors real and yet imperial,
water to fire, the envious gossiper.

AUTUMN

Autumn again. A wide-eyed absence in
the woods and skies. The trees once berry-ripe
are cleared of weight and in the midday shine,

forlorn perhaps. Triumphant. It is true
that exile, parting, is our earthly lot,
though roots cling tight below the green and blue.

O handkerchiefs wave free while the full heart
is squeezed of purple, leaving the wrinkled skin.
Depend on everything, depend on art,

your crystal table set with paper, pen,
such simple instruments. Begin once more.
Spring in its fury breaks on us again,

frizzle of summer, winter with its snow,
and also autumn beating the hazels down
from trees enriched by taste and by red hue.

Art feeds us, famished. It's the heavenly crown,
the earthly crown against the dazzling blue.

THE LEGEND

Today, receiving a letter from a friend
who was once a schoolmate, now in Canada,
I am returned to what seemingly I was.

'I remember talking to you, about Graham Greene,
for two hours together on a freezing day
in bleak November in the "Royal" doorway.

Another time, our cases soaked with salt,
from a stormy crossing, all that worried you
was whether all your poems were still dry.'

I can remember nothing. Was I like that?
The anthology of memories of the other
is a book I hadn't reckoned on. My fear

or rather hope is that I am put back
further and further in that clutch of tales
till I am lost for ever to these fables,

O false and lying and yet perhaps true.
I would be barer with no foliage round me,
without a title, a great blank behind me,

and only a real future ahead,
myself with a caseful of impersonal poems,
unsalted, bare, and floating out of my arms.

THE CHURCH

I imagine a gothic church
made of icicles
rising out of the Middle Ages.

Below it there are peasants with scythes
setting out in the morning
into the manuscripts of fields.

How dazzling the church is
with its fine detailed deaths
hung so precariously there.

And the nobles ride out on their horses
to hunt the wild boar,
threshing the cornfield,

while the gothic church looks down.
It remembers their bones,
it catalogues the blood in their breasts.

It remembers, hanging there,
in its inhuman music,
the arthritic hands at the plough
the bloodstained hand at the sword.

All is transmuted
into the tracery of memory
before the great sun bursts out
and melts its white towers.

POWER CUT

Suddenly there was darkness
and our hands were white in our laps,
and the words in the book died.

The pint of beer was hidden,
the saw lost its teeth,
and the cup vanished down a well.

If we should live in the dark
how our manners would change utterly,
how our poems would no longer be written,

but spoken from the wet roots
among the scurries of mice,
in the leafy classroom of owls,
by the light of the weasel.

The screams, the terrors, the notes
of the ungovernable music.
The great poet would be made of iron
hunched in the rain

and the tears would pour down his face forever.
He would be like a statue
over which no sun would rise,
no rainbow's pardoning bridge.

SNOW POEMS

1

Not through snow the ancient heroes walk,
not Hamlet or Othello or Ulysses,
it is in heat that tragedy is found.

When with snow on armour did Achilles
enter the kitchen of adversity,
or on his hair the maps of melting white?

For snow falls down from heaven, not from earth
exuding upwards does it stink of man,
or of his bones, his flesh, his intellect,

the wild yet rooted flash of jealousy,
or settled envy in its tract of green
or greed that steadily hungers for pale gold.

No, it is other. Quixote did not plod
with lance uplifted through a weight of snow
towards the rainbow of extremity.

It is more suited to far fairy-tales,
the pathos of the roofless, and the poor.
It is the cloak they pull about them in

the nineteenth century especially,
when people noticed snow, among the hulks
of ruined ships, and harsh industrialism,

whose outlines became softened by the snow
far from the ring in which pale Hector died
in snowless Troy, which was no toy of ice.

Much more than ghost or essence, much more palpable,
and not a riddle of philosophy,
the snow clings to the trees, adorns the roofs.

It is the real, the sparkling doppelganger,
twin of the body, cold that grasps our souls,
that dances with us on the naked ice.

It is the other side of all our hopes,
reflection and companion, spectral friend,
the grin that vanishes, the water changer,

and therefore to the magic world akin,
here now then gone without the grief of longing,
leaving no will behind it in the rain,

and not so human as the breath of roses,
beyond regret or joy, what simply is,
and then what simply was, and may return,

but not a growth that is inevitable,
more like a simple visitor or guest
who has left the house before the rest awake.

3

A rat-shaped smoky cloud in the sky
strangely hovering over the snowy church
as if it had risen from the earth below,

from an earth that's bare of motion and of leaf,
coloured intently white, unnatural.
The smoky shape is changing as it floats.

Perhaps it was once a fire that has gone out
or a sign of evil in the naked sky,
a wicked shade, that hates the Christmas church,

leaving behind it a long smoky spoor,
squatting on nothing, blatantly being there,
while the rest of the sky is empty and is blue,

with smoky teeth and claws, above that spire,
a smoky laughter of the universe,
the unconverted rat that never dies.

BREUGHEL

A bony horse with a bird on it droops its head.
With a cart of skulls like potatoes Death drives onward.

There's a storm of monsters, snouted and obscene,
and on another page a neat snow scene.

Large peasants dance under a leaden sky
and ships are sinking in a black-framed sea.

The blind raise tortured faces. In Cockayne
they eat and drink and sleep and at the moon

a peasant pisses. Proverbs multiply.
Children with adult faces gravely play

while aprons break the storm, red plates and jugs,
Death in a hood and lands pulled back like rugs.

And over the countryside the black birds go
with far below them hunters in the snow.

OWL AND MOUSE

The owl wafts home with a mouse in its beak.
The moon is stunningly bright in the high sky.

Such a gold stone, such a brilliant hard light.
Such large round eyes of the owl among the trees.

All seems immortal but for the dangling mouse,
an old hurt string among the harmony

of the masterful and jewelled orchestra
which shows no waste soundlessly playing on.

'IOLAIRE'

[On New Year's Eve 1918 a ship called the *Iolaire* left Kyle of Loch-alsh to bring three hundred men home to Lewis after the war was over. On New Year's morning 1919 the ship went on the rocks as a result of a navigational error at the Beasts of Holm, a short distance from Stornoway, the main town on the island. About two hundred sailors were drowned. In the following poem I imagine an elder of the church speaking as he is confronted with this mind-breaking event.]

The green washed over them. I saw them when
the New Year brought them home. It was a day
that orbed the horizon with an enigma.
It seemed that there were masts. It seemed that men
buzzed in the water round them. It seemed that fire
shone in the water which was thin and white
unravelling towards the shore. It seemed that I
touched my fixed hat which seemed to float and then
the sun illumined fish with naval caps,
names of the vanished ships. In sloppy waves,
in the fat of water, they came floating home
bruising against their island. It is true,
a minor error can inflict this death.
That star is not responsible. It shone
over the puffy blouse, the flapping blue
trousers, the black boots. The seagull swam
bonded to the water. Why not man?
The lights were lit last night, the tables creaked
with hoarded food. They willed the ship to port
in the New Year which would erase the old,
its errant voices, its unpractised tones.
Have we done ill, I ask, my fixed body
a simulacrum of the transient waste,
for everything was mobile, planks that swayed,
the keeling ship exploding and the splayed
cold insect bodies. I have seen your church

solid. This is not. The water pours
into the parting timbers where I ache
above the globular eyes. The slack heads turn
ringing the horizon without sound,
with mortal bells, a strange exuberant flower
unknown to our dry churchyards. I look up.
The sky begins to brighten as before,
remorseless amber, and the bruised blue grows
at the erupting edges. I have known you, God,
not as the playful one but as the black
thunderer from hills. I kneel
and touch this dumb blond head. My hand is scorched.
Its human quality confuses me.
I have not felt such hair so dear before
nor seen such real eyes. I kneel from you.
This water soaks me. I am running with
its tart sharp joy. I am floating here
in my black uniform. I am embraced
by these green ignorant waters. I am calm.

FOR POETS WRITING IN ENGLISH
OVER IN IRELAND

'Feeling,' they said,
'that's the important thing'—
those poets who write in English over in Ireland.

It was late.
There was dancing in the hall,
playing of pipes, of bones, of the penny whistle.

They were an island in that Irishness.
'Larkin and Dunn,' they said. 'Now Dunn is open
to more of the world than aging Larkin is.

What room was Mr Bleaney in? It's like
going to any tenement and finding
any name you can think of on the door.

And you wonder a little about him but not much.'
We were sitting on the floor outside the room
where a song in Irish waltzed the Irish round.

Do the stones, the sea, seem different in Irish?
Do we walk in language, in a garment pure
as water? Or as earth just as impure?

The grave of Yeats in Sligo, Innisfree
island seen shivering on an April day.
The nuns who cycle down an Easter road.

The days are beads strung on a thin wire.
Language at Connemara is stone
and the water green as hills is running westwards.

The little children in the primary school
giggling a little at our Scottish Gaelic,
writing in chalk the Irish word for 'knife'.

To enter a different room. When did Bleaney
dance to the bones? This world is another world.
A world of a different language is a world

we find our way about in with a stick,
half-deaf half-blind, snatching a half word there,
seeing a twisted figure in a mirror,

slightly unnerved, unsure. I must go home.
To English? Gaelic? O beautiful Maud Gonne,
the belling hounds spoke in what language to you?

In that tall tower so finished and so clear
his international name was on the door
and who would ask who had been there before him?

I turn a page and read an Irish poem
translated into English and it says
(the poet writing of his wife who'd died):

'Half of my eyes you were, half of my hearing,
half of my walking you were, half of my side.'
From what strange well are these strange words upspringing?

But then I see you, Yeats, inflexible will,
creator of yourself, a conscious lord,
writing in English of your own Maud Gonne.

Inside the room there's singing and there's dancing.
Another world is echoing with its own
music that's distant from the world of Larkin.

And I gaze at the three poets. They are me,
poised between two languages. They have chosen
with youth's superb confidence and decision.

'Half of my side you were, half of my seeing,
half of my walking you were, half of my hearing.'
Half of this world I am, half of this dancing.

THE SCHOOLMASTER

Sometimes I see the schoolmaster on the boat
that is shiny with brine, and comes from Asia.

He is the Ancient Mariner and his finger
jabs at a pamphlet soaked with salt,

the words running away from back to front,
the albatross outstretched, its eyes glazing.

The rickshaws arrive at the wedding, with the dead
piled high like paintings, and the wedding guest

ignorantly smoking his cigar.
'Shalom' they cry to the president on the throne.

The sea is boundless, of an alien blue.
The blackboard throbs with fire, in his old clothes

he is a shabby scarecrow. The sun is rising.
Hand in hand in front of the drenched altar

they watch the child with his swollen bubbling face.

LOST

Lost, we go from street to street
past the cinema showing *The Deer Hunter*.

They are playing Russian roulette,
red bandages on their eyes.

Where are we? Is it here or Saigon?

What street is this, that the soldiers are in the water with the
    rats.
Who are you, drunkard with the black cap,
swaying?

We want to go home. A safe wound will be enough.
He is putting the gun to his head.
The gooks are watching.

I think we are in a maze of green
and there is a rickshaw coming towards us
with Death in red riding in it.

He bows deeply. We are in the middle of his dead eyes
and the bloodstained chopper takes off.

HALLOWEEN

Someone was playing the piano when quite suddenly
there they were standing in the room.
They would not sing or speak or tell their names.
Their skull faces blankly shifted round
as if they were studying us implacably.
'Yokels,' one said. 'Rustics,' said another,
and truly they had come in out of the rain
with their masks tall and white and bony-looking.
'Macbeth,' someone said, and someone, 'Hamlet'.
Or perhaps at least the 'Elegy' by Gray.
The rain drummed on the roof and they were gone
in their muddy boots, squelching past cowering doors.
We looked at each other. It was graveyard time
as our black ties on our white shirts might say.

POEM

It is always evening in a German poem,
the moon shining on the shell-like houses
and the roses like swans' necks bowed over lakes.

Something is always about to happen,
a crouched being rising over the horizon
with fur on its hands and fur about its cheeks.

Past the water it comes, out of the moonlight,
heading steadily past the little church,
the tavern that resounds with loud tunes.

And it stands, turning its head in the moonlight,
slowly, purposefully, in the pure light
among the roses with the necks of swans

while somewhere in the distance a bell rings
very gently, humbly, and a milkmaid
sings to herself, the warm pail in her hand.

THE SURVIVORS

How can they survive the days
those who have no talent
how can they face the sharpness of the morning star?

Those who have no direction
who have nothing they can do well
whose days do not form a book

or even a particular style
such that it feeds on the clouds
and on the big spaces between them.

Admire them most of all
those who built the pyramids
but were too close to them to see.

Those who died
before the road was completed
before the bridge spanned the water.

The hyphens the dashes the strokes—
those who see the sunsets
as wheels that return and return.

These I think are the true heroes,
they push stones away from their breasts
when they rise in the morning.

THE 'ORDINARY' PEOPLE

The 'ordinary' people sing on the edge of the grave.
When the hero howls and cries they are humming
in the middle of ropes, griefs, the deaths of roses.

The 'ordinary' people are not stones.
They are revengeful, bitter, quick to strike and laugh
and they buy oranges at the market-place.

The 'ordinary' people say, 'I'll not be put upon.'
They spend their money freely on food and drink
and then they have no money, only hope.

Where does the hope come from that they see,
who live precariously by the deaths of roses,
and hang their washing among tragedies?

I begin to think there are no 'ordinary' people.

Or rather that they've learned about tragedies
from birth and can simply pass them by
or walk through them clutching food, bottles.

I believe there is no such thing as tragedy,
that the hero has deceived us, is the red infant
howling and screaming from his wooden cage.

AT THE FUNERAL OF ROBERT GARIOCH

Something about the April day
touched me
as they slid your coffin onto the trolley
in the Crematorium.

More and more often it troubles me
this wind my sails have missed
which is still around me
fluttering the bluebells.

'The Lord's My Shepherd' we sang.
It was time for the burning.
The minister blessed it
dressed in his white gown,

his voice fat and voluptuous,
his enunciation pure.
You slid down into fire
in your yellow coffin.

In half-way April
the breeze was vulnerable
straying among the warble
of the first birds.

Poet, the flowers open
even when we are dead
even when the power has gone
from our right arms.

The flowers open in flame.
The coffin slides home.
Fugitive April becomes
a tremendous summer.

WHO DAILY

Who daily at the rickety table
writes and sings, writes and sings,
Venus with the one arm,
Apollo with the one leg,
the stuttering rainbow that hirples
like early crayons into the sea.

ENVOI

There are
more things in heaven and earth, Horatio,
than bones, roses. There are windows
through which gaunt faces peer
and there are children
running through great doors.

Consider
how the sea roars mournfully at the edge of
all things, how the seaweed
hangs at the sailor's neck, the crab
shuffles in armour. Horatio,
the punctual dead visit us, rise
bird-voiced from the grass,
and the owls
are scholars of the woods.
Horatio, I remember
a kingdom and a kingdom's diplomat,
a girl floating tenderly down stream,
a crown on her young head.
These are portents, warnings, ominous
reflections from the mirror.
Horatio
my eyes darken. Tragedy is
nothing but churned foam.
I wave to you
from this secure and leafy entrance,
this wooden
door on which I bump my head,
this moment and then,
that.

SOME CARCANET TITLES OF SCOTTISH INTEREST

J. F. HENDRY/THE SACRED THRESHOLD: A LIFE OF RILKE

G. S. FRASER/A STRANGER AND AFRAID: AUTOBIOGRAPHY

ROBERT GARIOCH/COLLECTED POEMS

FRANK KUPPNER/A BAD DAY FOR THE SUNG DYNASTY

EDWIN MORGAN/POEMS OF THIRTY YEARS

EDWIN MORGAN/THE NEW DIVAN

BURNS SINGER/SELECTED POEMS

Anthologies

THOMAS CRAWFORD/LOVE, LABOUR & LIBERTY

MAURICE LINDSAY/MODERN SCOTTISH POETRY

EDWIN MORGAN/RITES OF PASSAGE

EDWIN MORGAN/SCOTTISH SATIRICAL VERSE

Fyfield Books

ROBERT HENRYSON/SELECTED POEMS

CARCANET POETS INCLUDE

JOHN ASH
JOHN ASHBERY
CLIFF ASHBY
EDMUND BLUNDEN
CHARLES BOYLE
ALISON BRACKENBURY
KEITH CHANDLER
GILLIAN CLARKE
ANNE CLUYSENAAR
PATRICK CREAGH
MICHAEL CULLUP
ELIZABETH DARYUSH
DONALD DAVIE
JEAN EARLE
PADRAIC FALLON
ROBERT GARIOCH
H.D. (Hilda Doolittle)
MICHAEL HAMBURGER
ROBERT HASS
JOHN HEATH-STUBBS
JEREMY HOOKER
PETER JAY
ELIZABETH JENNINGS
BRIAN JONES
PETER JONES
DENNIS KEENE
FRANK KUPPNER

WYNDHAM LEWIS
IAN McMILLAN
CHARLOTTE MEW
CHRISTOPHER MIDDLETON
PAUL MILLS
EDWIN MORGAN
ANDREW MOTION
JOHN PECK
ROBERT PINSKY
NEIL POWELL
GARETH REEVES
I. A. RICHARDS
LAURA (RIDING) JACKSON
MICHAEL ROBERTS
DELMORE SCHWARTZ
BURNS SINGER
C. H. SISSON
IAIN CRICHTON SMITH
ADRIAN STOKES
MICHAEL VINCE
JEFFREY WAINWRIGHT
SYLVIA TOWNSEND WARNER
ANDREW WATERMAN
ROBERT WELLS
CLIVE WILMER
YVOR WINTERS
DAVID WRIGHT

For a full catalogue, including details of our new poetry, fiction, translations, 'Lives & Letters' and Fyfield Books, write to us at

CARCANET PRESS
208-212 Corn Exchange Buildings
Manchester M4 3BQ